Jungle Party

Brian Wildsmith

EGMONT

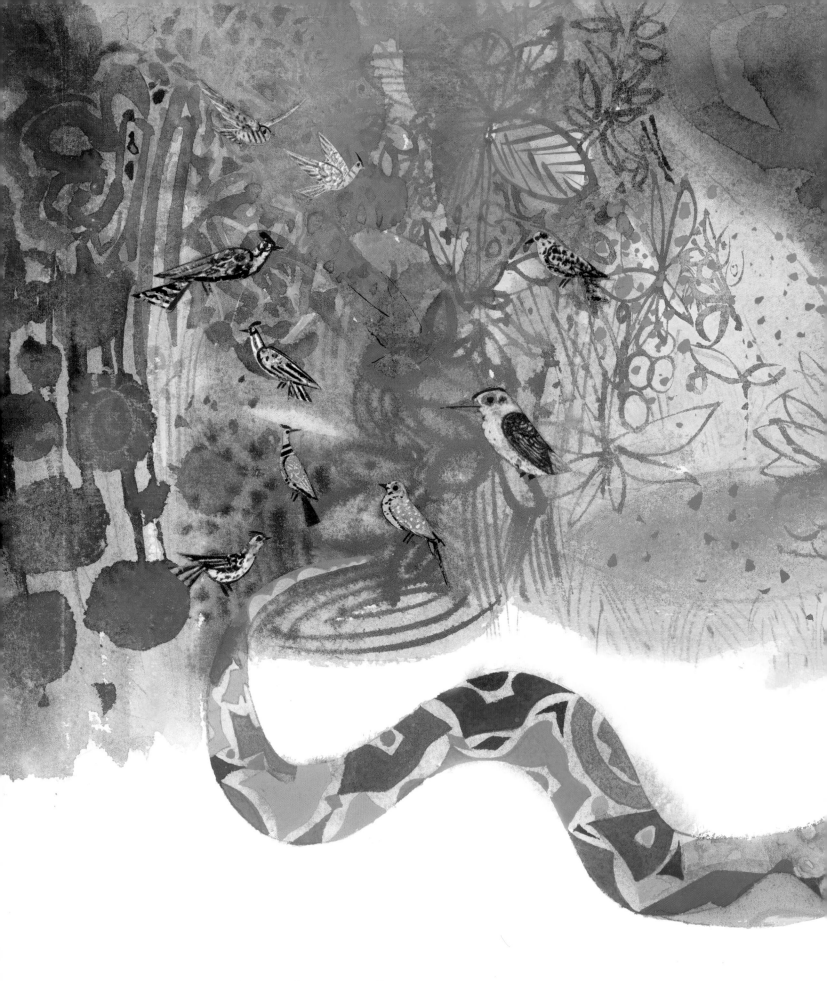

Deep in the jungle, Python was hungry.
Although he hunted every day for food, he could not find any
because all the animals hid themselves from him.

Jungle Party

For Aurélie

First published by Oxford University Press in 1974
First published in this edition by Egmont UK Limited in 2006
239 Kensington High Street, London W8 6SA

Text and illustrations copyright © Brian Wildsmith 1974

The author has asserted his moral rights

ISBN-10   1 4052 2154 2 (Hardback)
ISBN-13   978 1 4052 2154 2 (Hardback)
ISBN-10   1 4052 2155 0 (Paperback)
ISBN-13   978 1 4052 2155 9 (Paperback)

10 9 8 7 6 5 4 3 2

A CIP catalogue record for this title is available from the British Library

Colour Reproductions by Dot Gradations Ltd, UK
Printed and bound in Italy

After a whole week of hunger,
Python thought of a cunning scheme.

He climbed a tree, and called out:
> *"Friends, I know you are hiding, but don't be afraid.*
> *I promise to be good, and to show you that I mean it,*
> *I invite you all to my party."*

The animals crept near to the tree – but they all felt nervous and were ready
to run if the Python started to come down.

Python called down again.

"*On my honour, I promise to behave myself.*
Everyone will be safe at my party."

Goat and Fox thought they ought to believe him, and anyway they liked parties.

So they persuaded the others, and everyone accepted Python's invitation.
Python slithered down the tree, full of ideas for the party.

"Let's have a competition to see

who can do the cleverest tricks," he shouted.

"I'll be master of ceremonies," cried Parrot,

"and announce what each one

is going to do."

So the animals sat down and thought hard
          about the tricks that they would perform,

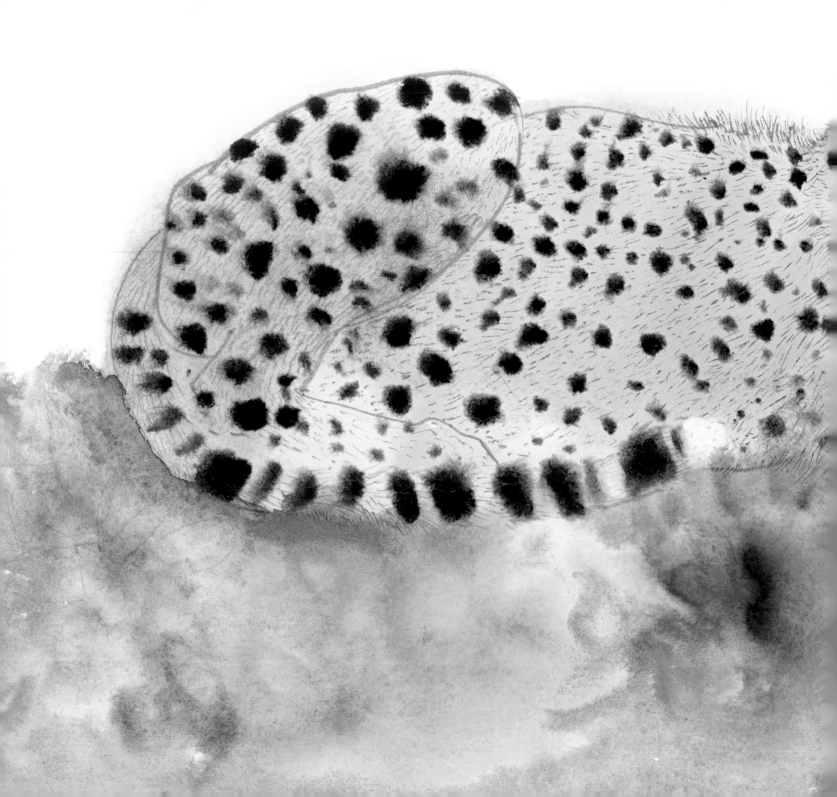

and when they were ready Parrot went around
so that they could whisper in his ear.

Then
the party
began.

Parrot cried out:

"The first trick is to be given by Gnu and the jungle fowl,
with a little help from Chameleon."

The audience watched,
and shouted,

**"Not bad.
Not bad."**

And clapped as loud as they could.

"And now for a feat never before seen in this jungle. The world-famous Hyena will walk on two round melons for a distance of twenty yards!"

The audience were very impressed, and held their breath while Hyena wobbled along.

"That's great,"
they said.
"That trick will
be hard
to beat."

"Now for an act of strength and balance
by none other than the spotted leopard
and four agile monkeys."

"**Wow!**" said the audience.
"**These tricks get better
and better.**"

"Quiet now for my lord Lion," cried Parrot.
Lion, who had been behind some bushes dabbing himself with mud, now stepped proudly forward.
"You can have three guesses
at what I am supposed to be," he said.

"A lion pretending to be a leopard."
"No," sniffed Lion.
"A domino!"
Lion looked puzzled. He had never heard of a domino before.
"A lion with dirt on him," called out a baby guinea fowl.
Lion roared with laughter.
"No. I am a lion with measles!"

"Now for a double act," Parrot put in quickly, because he thought the audience looked rather huffed. "Fox and Genet will now entertain us."

The audience cheered up and clapped and stamped their feet.

"Good, good," they shouted.

Parrot forgot what Zebra was going to do,
but Zebra did not wait to be announced anyway.

He balanced coconuts on his back hoofs, threw them up in the air, and as they came down, kicked them into little pieces.

"That's wonderful,"
the audience cried
and scuffled about excitedly.

Parrot was nearly as excited as the audience, and he rather muddled up his announcement of the last act.
"Our fine feathered friend, Pelican, will endeavour to collect as many fine feathered friends – I mean as many friends – with or without feathers – as many friends as possible into his beak."

Pelican had fixed it up beforehand with some members of the audience and they rushed out to climb into his capacious mouth.

"**My word,**" the rest of the animals breathed, in awe.

"That really takes some beating."

Python stretched himself and smiled.

"Oh, I don't know," he said modestly.
*"I believe I can do better than that. I could get more
of you into my mouth than Pelican."*

By this time everyone was too excited to be cautious.

"All right," they said.
"If you think so,
you have a try."

So Python opened his mouth wide, and they all began
to climb into it.

Soon some of them decided that they didn't like it inside Python.

"All right, you win," they called out from one end of Python to the other.
"It's dark in here and we would like to come out now."

Python closed his mouth with a snap.
    "I'm sorry," he said, in a hissing voice.
        "But now that I have you, I mean to keep you.
                I have been hungry
                  for long enough."

When they realized that they had been tricked, the animals began to shout,
but Python was not disturbed and lay down to enjoy a snooze.
He had no sooner dropped off than Elephant came by, and heard the
shouting from inside the sleeping snake. The animals knew it was he
by his heavy tread.

"Elephant, Python has tricked us and we are all
                    shut up inside here and can't get out,"
they called, in muffled and tearful voices.

Elephant did not waste his words.
Instead, he lifted his foot and
stamped hard
on Python's tail.

Python woke up with a start,
and opened his mouth with a shout of pain.

Immediately the animals began to tumble out as fast as possible,

and Elephant kept his foot firmly on Python's tail

until the last one had escaped.

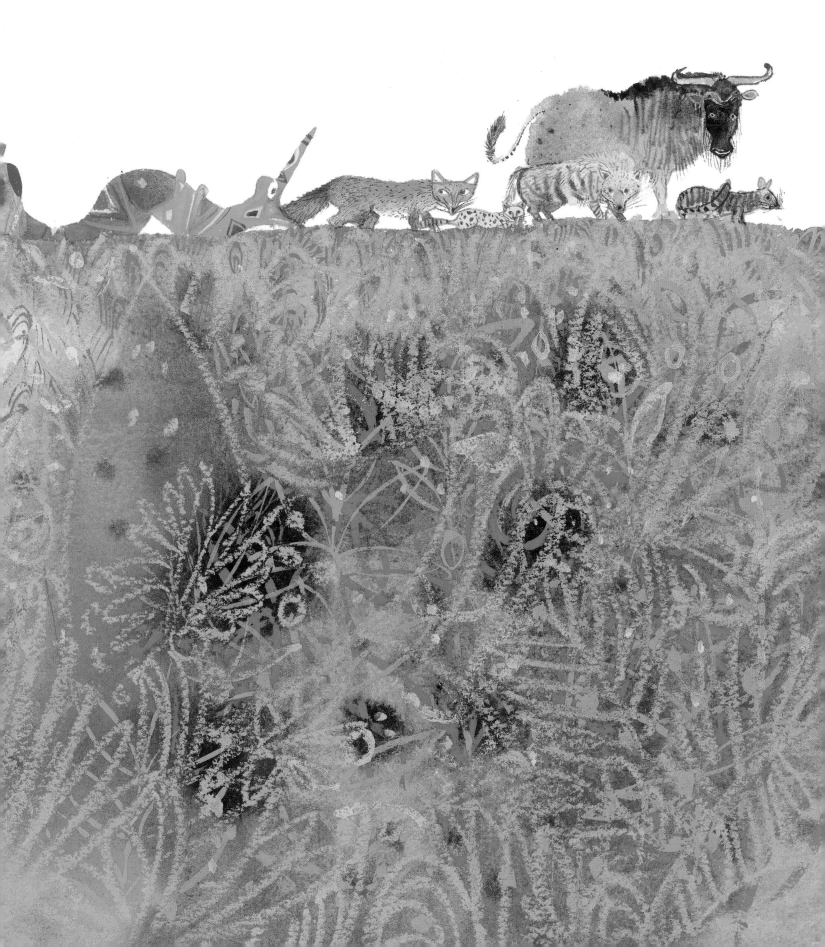

"**That was a very nasty trick,**" the animals told Python.
And while Elephant stood guard, they tied a knot in Python's tail.
"**That is to remind you,**" they said severely,

"**not to do it again.**"

"And let it remind you too,"
Elephant said to the animals, "never to play with Python,
even at his own party."

But the animals said they wouldn't need a knot
to remind them never again to go to
a party given by a python.